Margaret K. McElderry Books
Macmillan Publishing Company
866 Third Avenue
New York, NY 10022
First published 1991 in Great Britain by Pan Macmillan
Children's Books, London
First American edition 1992

Printed and bound in Hong Kong
10 9 8 7 6 5 4 3 2 1

Library of Congress Cataloging-in-Publication Data
Thomson, Pat, date
Beware of the aunts! / Pat Thomson ; illustrated by Emma
Chichester Clark. — 1st American ed.
p.   cm.
"First published 1991 in Great Britain by Pan Macmillan Children's
Books, London"—T.p. verso.
"Margaret K. McElderry Books"—T.p. verso.
Summary: A little girl lists the foibles of her nine eccentric
aunts, from the constantly kissing Aunt Anne to Aunt Jane and her
amazing hats.
ISBN 0-689-50538-8
[1. Aunts—Fiction.]   I. Clark, Emma Chichester, ill.   II. Title.
PZ7.T3766Be   1992   90-28928
[E]—dc20

BEWARE OF THE AUNTS!

Pat Thomson

Illustrated by
Emma Chichester Clark

MARGARET K. McELDERRY BOOKS
New York

MAXWELL MACMILLAN INTERNATIONAL PUBLISHING GROUP
New York   Oxford   Singapore   Sydney

My family is not very big. I have a little sister and a big brother. I have a mother, a father, a cat, a dog, and a goldfish.

Mom and Dad both come from big families. I have two grandmothers and one grandfather. I don't mind them at all. But I'll tell you what the big problem is. My mother has lots of sisters. My father has even more sisters.

That means I have too many aunts.

Aunt Anne is far too fond of kissing. Dad goes out when she comes around, but she always kisses Mom. She hugs and kisses my big brother. She kisses me and says, "How you've grown!" My poor little sister is showered with kisses.

She even kisses the cat.

Aunt Betty eats a lot. She once ate ten helpings of ice cream. She never takes just one sandwich.

She always helps herself to the largest slice of cake. She even took the last cookie on the plate.

She's staying with us now.

The dog's biscuits are missing.

Aunt Elizabeth must be very rich. She wears a fur coat.

The dog growls at her when she comes in. She says that it's not real fur, that it's only a fun-fur coat.

But she was cross when we had some fun with it in the hall.

Aunt Zara likes to sew. She makes all her own clothes.

Dad says you can tell she does. I think she must like very bright colors. She once made a dress out of a bedspread. She kept tripping over the fringe.

She sometimes makes *us* things.

My Aunt Mary is very kind. The only thing wrong with her is my cousin Rodney. Rodney wins medals for ballroom dancing.

He is always clean and neat. He likes being with grown-ups and handing around tea in the garden.

He slipped and fell into the garden pond once.

Aunt Jean is really fussy about her house. We hate going there.

We have to wash our hands all the time. Her kitchen is like a hospital. Her floor is like a skating rink.

No children are allowed in her best room.

We haven't been there to visit since our dog had a fight with her tablecloth.

Aunt Susan always forgets her glasses.

"Hello, little poppet," she says to my big brother.
She once put a saucer of milk on the floor for my little
sister, tried to feed the television set with fish food,
and thought the cat was her scarf.

That was the day she went out wearing her best coat and the lampshade from the hall lamp.

I'm almost sure Aunt Charlotte is a witch.

I've seen her wearing a big, black cloak. Her nails are long and red. Her black cat scratched me once.

She lives down a lane in a cottage with strange herbs hanging from the kitchen beams.

There's a frog in her garden.
I wonder who it really is?

Aunt Jane loves new hats—fur ones in the winter,

flowery ones in the summer. We are not allowed to laugh.

But the one with a parrot on top makes her look like a pirate. Dad says all she needs is a wooden leg!

At Christmas they all come and visit us. They talk and talk. The house is full of aunts. There are aunts in the kitchen, aunts in the bathroom, aunts in the bedrooms. Dad says we should put down aunt powder. It's really awful. But on the other hand . . .

you can't have too many aunts
at Christmas!